Nathan's Hanukkah Bargain

Nathan's Hanukkah Bargain

Jacqueline Dembar Greene

Illustrated by Judith Hierstein

Affectionately dedicated to all our grandpas,
because they always understand.
—J. D. G.

The word "Pelican" and the depiction of a pelican
are trademarks of Pelican Publishing Company, Inc.,
and are registered in the U.S. Patent and Trademark Office.

Library of Congress Cataloging-in-Publication Data

Greene, Jacqueline Dembar.
  Nathan's Hanukkah bargain / by Jacqueline Dembar Greene / illustrated by Judith Hierstein.
      p. cm.
  Summary: Nathan's unsuccessful search for a Hanukkah menorah takes a new turn when his Grandpa teaches him about old-fashioned bargaining.
   ISBN-13: 978-1-58980-454-8 (hardcover : alk. paper) [1. Hanukkah—Fiction 2. Grandfathers—Fiction] I. Hierstein, Judy, ill. II. Title.
   PZ7.G834Nat 2008
   [E]—dc22
                                    2008004122

Printed in Korea
Published by Pelican Publishing Company, Inc.
1000 Burmaster Street, Gretna, Louisiana 70053

NATHAN'S HANUKKAH BARGAIN

Nathan carefully placed the last quarter atop the stack of coins lined up on the kitchen table.

"Five dollars!" he announced. "Will you take me shopping, Grandpa?"

"You must need a few last-minute Hanukkah gifts," Grandpa guessed. Nathan dropped the quarters into his pocket.

"I already have presents for everyone," he said, "but there's something I want to buy for myself." He zipped his jacket. "Come on, Grandpa. Let's go before the stores close."

Grandpa pulled himself up from his comfortable chair and got his hat and coat. "So," he said as they walked down the stairs, "with a king's ransom in your pocket, what is it that you must have? A new sled? A robot that changes shape?"

Nathan shook his head. "Not a toy, Grandpa. I want a Hanukkah menorah for my very own." Grandpa gave Nathan's hand a squeeze, and Nathan knew he approved.

"Even a pocketful of quarters might not be enough," Grandpa said. "Let me give you a few dollars." He reached for his wallet.

"Thanks, Grandpa, but I want to buy this myself. I'm sure I saved up enough."

Grandpa pointed to a shop at the end of the block. "There's one store that might have what you're looking for." Nathan ran to the window and looked at the bright display of books and gifts.

Inside, the store was crowded. Israeli music played over the sound system. Grownups browsed for books, and children poked through bins filled with colorful dreidels. Grandpa led Nathan to the shelves of Hanukkah menorahs.

"May I help you?" a saleswoman asked Grandpa.

"My grandson is the shopper today," he explained.

The woman smiled at Nathan. "What kind of menorah would you like?"

Nathan hesitated. "I'm not sure. I didn't know there would be so many."

"How about an electric one?" the clerk suggested. She took down a brass lamp with orange light bulbs. "This can be safely placed in the window," she said.

Nathan frowned. "I like to see a real flame. That's the best part."

"How about one that holds candles?" the clerk asked. She reached for a green enameled menorah with twisting branches. Grandpa crinkled his nose as if he smelled something awful.

"That's too modern," Nathan said politely. He thought for a moment. "Do you have one that burns oil, like in the days of the Maccabees?"

"Oh, something traditional," said the sales clerk. She showed Nathan a menorah shaped like the Western Wall in Jerusalem. It was made of mosaic tiles and had nine tiny clay pots for burning oil. The price tag read, "$65."

"That's too expensive," Nathan said.

"I think I have just the thing," the clerk declared. She took out a menorah no bigger than Nathan's hand. "This comes all the way from Israel and holds ordinary birthday candles. It's only three dollars."

Nathan was disappointed. "No thanks," he said, pulling Grandpa toward the door.

Outside in the cold air, Nathan tried to think clearly. "Do you understand what I'm looking for, Grandpa?"

Grandpa nodded. "Sure. You need to find an old-fashioned menorah, the kind they made before all these artistic and electrified models came along."

"That's exactly it!" Nathan agreed. Grandpa did understand.

"You've still got a king's ransom," Grandpa reminded him, "and there's one more shop."

The next store wasn't much different than the first. Nathan looked at one menorah after another. They were either too expensive or not quite right.

Grandpa headed for a bench on the sidewalk. "Let's rest for a minute," he suggested.

Nathan's shoulders slumped. "I didn't know it would be so hard find the right one," he said, "and I didn't know menorahs cost so much."

"It's too bad you can't bargain in these stores," Grandpa sighed. "When I was a boy, peddlers sold things from a cart. There were no price tags. The peddler gave a price, but he expected the customer to offer less. Much less." He laughed, remembering. "Then the peddler's price came down a bit, and yours went up a bit. You would complain. The peddler would complain. But pretty soon you'd make a deal. A fair bargain meant the peddler was satisfied, and you felt like a smart buyer. It's just not the same anymore."

Nathan imagined the sidewalk full of peddlers. It was an interesting idea, but it wasn't going to help him buy a menorah today. As they walked home, Nathan wondered how he would ever find the right one.

Suddenly, Nathan tugged Grandpa's sleeve. "Look!" he cried, pointing to a basement window. "There it is!"

Grandpa peered into a cluttered shop window. Leaning against a torn lampshade was a tarnished menorah.

"A menorah in a junk shop!" he marveled.

Nathan jumped to the bottom of the stairs and pushed open the door. A bell tinkled softly. The antique store was dim, and there were no other customers.

"Buying or browsing?" came a voice from behind them. Nathan was startled. He turned to see a man bundled in a tweed coat and scarf, wearing gloves without fingers. A stubble of gray beard sprouted on his face.

"I'd like to see the Hanukkah menorah in the window," Nathan stammered.

"Eh?" said the man. "Menorah?" He shuffled forward, pushing boxes and broken chairs out of his way. He squinted at the jumbled heap.

"Over there," Nathan pointed. "Next to the lampshade."

The shopkeeper reached into the window, knocking over several chipped dishes. He plunked the menorah onto a scratched oak desk littered with papers.

"Twelve dollars," he announced. Nathan turned to go.

Grandpa leaned down and whispered, "Bargain!" Then he settled into a worn armchair.

How can I bargain? Nathan wondered. He had never done it before. He tried to remember what Grandpa had told him about peddlers.

Nathan wanted the menorah more than anything, but maybe he shouldn't let the shopkeeper know.

He eyed the man coolly. "It has a dent."

"Dent, shment," the shopkeeper mocked. "It's pure silver. It's a steal at ten dollars."

Bargaining was an interesting game, Nathan thought, but maybe it wouldn't work. The menorah was beautiful, with a long graceful stem and nine little cups just waiting to be filled with oil. It was nicer than all the new ones he had seen.

"It's nearly black," Nathan argued. "I'll give you three dollars for it."

"Three dollars?" the shopkeeper gasped. "Why, this menorah survived the Russian Revolution! I won't consider a penny less than eight dollars."

Nathan turned the menorah over and saw faint markings on the bottom. They looked like Russian letters.

"If that's true," he said, "I'll give you four dollars."

"It's handmade," the man sputtered. "There isn't another like it in the entire world. Seven dollars is my final offer."

Nathan thought the bargaining was going well. The shopkeeper had lowered the price quite a bit, but Nathan still didn't have enough money.

"Take it or leave it," the shopkeeper said.

Nathan shrugged. "I guess I'll leave it," he replied. He turned toward the door and gave Grandpa a sly wink.

"I give up," the man sighed, raising his hands in surrender. "Better you should have it than it should sit in my dusty window. Five dollars, and I don't want to hear another word!"

"Sold!" Nathan exclaimed. He reached into his pocket and counted out five neat stacks of quarters.

Nathan imagined how the menorah would look after he polished it to a shine. He would bet Grandpa knew someone who could read the Russian letters.

Outside, Grandpa slapped Nathan on the back. "What a bargain! I could have used your help when I was a boy. Just think what a story you'll have to tell your grandchildren."

Nathan smiled. "I'll tell them how you helped me. I couldn't have done it if you hadn't told me about bargaining."

Nathan tucked his treasure under his arm and gave Grandpa's hand a squeeze. Nathan knew he'd understand.

About Hanukkah

In Jerusalem more than two thousand years ago, Judah Maccabee and his supporters fought for the right to practice their religion of Judaism. After their victory, the Jews purified their temple. When they tried to light the eternal lamp, they found only enough oil to last one day. Amazingly, the light burned for eight days, long enough for more oil to be made. Today, Jews around the world celebrate Hanukkah each year to remember the survival of their religion and the re-dedication of their temple. They light oil or candles in a special eight-branched holder called a menorah. One light is added each night until the menorah is fully lit on the eighth night of the winter holiday.